Lincolnshire
COUNTY COUNCIL

COMMUNITIES, CULTURAL SERVICES
and ADULT EDUCATION

This book should be returned on or before the last date shown below.

To renew or order library books please telephone 01522 782010
or visit www.lincolnshire.gov.uk
You will require a Personal Identification Number.
Ask any member of staff for this.

EC. 199 (LIBS): RS/L5/19

First published in 2008 by
Franklin Watts
338 Euston Road
London
NW1 3BH

Franklin Watts Australia
Level 17/207 Kent Street
Sydney
NSW 2000

A CIP catalogue record for this book is available
from the British Library.

ISBN 978 0 7496 7889 0 (hbk)
ISBN 978 0 7496 7895 1 (pbk)

Series Editor: Jackie Hamley
Series Advisor: Dr Hilary Minns
Series Designer: Peter Scoulding

Printed in China

Franklin Watts is a division of
Hachette Children's Books,
an Hachette Livre UK company.

Amazing Shane

by Joan Stimson

Illustrated by Rob Hefferan

W

FRANKLIN WATTS

LONDON • SYDNEY

Joan Stimson

"I love watching the sheep in the field near my house, especially the ones that are just like Shane!"

Rob Hefferan

"Little Florence and I both hope that you enjoy reading this book as much as we enjoyed drawing the pictures!"

Shane the sheep lives on the hill.

Shane the sheep
is never still.

7

Shane the sheep
can leap a gate.

Amazing Shane
can spin a plate.

Shane the sheep
can kick a ball.

Amazing Shane
skips on the wall.

15

Shane the sheep
can climb a tree ...

17

... hang upside-down
and bleat with glee!

19

"It's never dull,"
says Farmer Wayne.

"For all my sheep
are just like Shane!"

23

Notes for adults

TADPOLES are structured to provide support for newly independent readers. The stories may also be used by adults for sharing with young children.

Starting to read alone can be daunting. **TADPOLES** help by providing visual support and repeating words and phrases. These books will both develop confidence and encourage reading and rereading for pleasure.

If you are reading this book with a child, here are a few suggestions:

1. Make reading fun! Choose a time to read when you and the child are relaxed and have time to share the story.
2. Talk about the story before you start reading. Look at the cover and the blurb. What might the story be about? Why might the child like it?
3. Encourage the child to reread the story, and to retell the story in their own words, using the illustrations to remind them what has happened.
4. Discuss the story and see if the child can relate it to their own experience, or perhaps compare it to another story they know.
5. Give praise! Remember that small mistakes need not always be corrected.

If you enjoyed this book, why not try another TADPOLES story?